Keith Yates

Hard Tune

Play Me like a Guitar

Hot Gay Romance Erotica

About the Publisher

4Fun Publishing, a member of **BLVNP Incorporated,** 340 S. Lemon #6200, Walnut CA 91789, info@blvnp.com / legal@blvnp.com
NOTE: Due to the highly emotional reaction of some people to works of erotic fiction, any email sent to the above address that contains foul language or religious references is automatically deleted by our anti-spam software and will not be seen. All other communications are welcome.

DISCLAIMER

Please don't be stupid and kill yourself. This book is a work of FICTION. Do not try any new sexual practice that you find in this book. It is fiction and not to be confused with reality. Neither the author nor the publisher or its associates assume any responsibility for any loss, injury, death or legal consequences resulting from acting on the contents in this book. Every character in this book is over 18 years of age. The author's opinions are not to be construed as the opinions of the publisher. The material in this book is for entertainment purposes ONLY. Enjoy.

The Hotel, Book 1

HARD TUNE

Play Me Like a Guitar

Hot Gay Romance Erotica

By: Keith Yates

© **Keith Yates 2014**
ISBN: 978-1-62761-873-1

HE CARRIED his overnight bag through the gilded door and nodded to acknowledge the well-built doorman. His steps took him quickly across the carpeted lobby to the check-in desk.

"Welcome back, sir," the well-dressed clerk said.

"Thank you. I have been looking forward to staying here again," he said, placing his bag on the floor.

"We always try our best to give our guests what they want. I believe you will find what we have for you to your liking."

"I am glad to hear it. I was hoping you would be able to, um, honor my request. I know it was a little more, um, of a special nature."

"It was but I think we found just the thing to satisfy you."

Removing his wallet from his jeans pocket, he passed the clerk his American Express. The clerk quickly swiped the card through the reader and passed it back to the very attractive man. Then the clerk picked up the phone and pressed a couple numbers and then said into the mouth piece, "Please send Chad out."

In only a couple of minutes, a young man stepped out of a door behind the clerk. His hair was blonde and curled around his ears. His face was lightly tanned and his eyes were a blue green color. They actually seemed to shift between blue and green as the young man walked around the desk.

"Chad, please escort Mr. Parsons to suite 800. Make sure you give him every courtesy."

"Yes, sir," the young man said, his voice nervous as he took the keycard from the clerk. "Right this way, sir."

BART PARSONS could not believe how attractive this young man was. He knew the kid had to be 18 but he looked younger. He looked 16 or 17 at the oldest. He wondered where they had found this clean-cut boy. He wondered if the boy's sun-kissed tan was a natural allover tan. Bart watched the young guy walk in front of him leading him to the elevators. He watched the tight black pants cling to the teen's firm bubble butt. Each of Chad's cheeks was squeezed by the delicate fabric. Bart wondered if the kid was wearing underwear.

They stepped into the elevator together and Chad hit the button for the 8th floor. He listened to the chimes of the elevator as they rode up in silence.

Bart's eyes took in the narrow waist of the kid and the way the silk shirt clung to the chest and arms of the boy. It was tailor-made to fit him and made to emphasize the boy's body. His shoulders and chest were defined by the shiny fabric and it clung to him in all the right places.

Bart's eyes slid down and checked out the young man's basket. It looked like the kid was slightly aroused. Bart would enjoy seeing just how aroused this boy could become.

"Right this way, sir," Chad said after stepping off the elevator.

Chad led Bart down the hall to a room at the end. Chad slipped the key card into the lock and pushed the door open while carrying Bart's bag through the doorway.

"This is very nice," Bart said, looking around the large suite. His eyes taking in the big bed through the doorway. The sitting room was well furnished and the large plasma TV was state-of-the-art. He could not ask for a more elaborate room.

"The, um, bar is fully stocked," Chad said, his voice nervous as he put Bart's suitcase in the bedroom. "Would you like to fix you a drink…I mean would you like me to fix you a drink?"

Bart grinned at the kid's nervousness. Bart knew this was going to be a fun stay. "Sure. Do you know how to fix a Manhattan?"

"Um, yes, sir. I believe so." Chad moved to the wet bar and took down a glass. He then bent to get vermouth and whiskey. He thought he could feel Bart's eyes watching him. He thought he could feel the man's eyes drinking in his firm round butt and the way the pants clung to each cheek.

With the kids' back to him, Bart reached down and rubbed a hand over the front of his blue jeans. His semi-erect member was stretching out the front of the denim material.

Chad returned with the drink in hand and noticed the bulge in the front of Bart's pants. He swallowed and took a few steps closer to Bart. His own body was tensing up at the man's obvious arousal. "Here you go, Mr. Parsons. I hope you find it to your liking."

"Oh, I am sure it is to my liking," Bart said, grinning as he took the drink from the kid's slightly trembling hand.

Chad watched Bart take a drink from the glass. He watched the arm flex and the bicep pop out as he lifted the glass to his lips. Chad had to admit that this was one of the hottest men he had seen come through the lobby. He couldn't believe he had been given a guest of this magnitude. Brent had said that guys usually started out with a lower class of guests before moving up to the big names. Maybe Bart Parsons was not considered a big name. It wasn't like he was a movie star, but he was still a big time celebrity.

"Very nice," Bart said after tasting the drink. "Where did you learn to make such a good drink?"

"I, um, my um, well, um it is part of our training."

Bart smiled to himself at how nervous this kid was. He couldn't believe how lucky he was to get such an obviously sweet and inexperienced attendant. "Can you tell me how long you have been working here?"

"Um, just a few weeks…you are…" Chad's voice trailed off. He had just been about to tell this man that he was the first guest he had been assigned to, but he didn't know if that would insult the celeb. He could not afford to be fired by ticking off a returning customer. "You're the first country music star I have been given the chance to help." Chat was proud of the way he had corrected what he was going to say. He thought he had done a nice job of saving his ass.

"Oh, and do you have a lot of country entertainers staying here?"

"Um, well, um, I, um…" Chad had known of a couple others. He had seen them passing through but he knew he couldn't tell Bart anything about another guest. It was strictly against the rules to divulge any information about a guest. "Well, you are the only one here today."

Bart let his eyes slide over the young man again. He couldn't believe how attractive the kid was. His body seemed to be in perfect proportion. The narrow waist, the shoulders and chest tapering down like a triangle... the long legs that made the boy only about 4 or 5 inches shorter than Bart.

"I, um, should go hang your clothes up. I don't want them to get wrinkled," Chad said nervously and quickly moved to the bedroom.

Bart watched the kid through the open bedroom door unpacking his suitcase. He saw the kid place his toiletries in the bathroom and then begin to unpack the clothes. Bart took another sip from the large Manhattan the kid had fixed and then moved into the bedroom. Chad's back was to the door as Bart stepped silently into the room. Bart moved up behind Chad and put his arms around the young man.

Chad jumped and almost caused Bart to spill the drink he held in one hand. His lips were close to Chad's ear and Chad could feel Bart's warm moist breath.

"Sorry I did not mean to scare you," Bart said into Chad's ear.

"I, um, you just well, um startled me."

"Don't worry, Chad, just relax," Bart said. "I think we are going to be good friends."

"I, I, um, hope so, Mr. Parsons ."

"Here, have a drink of this," Bart said moving the glass he had been drinking from to Chad's lips, "And please call me Bart."

"Um, yes, sir. Um, Bart."

Bart lifted the glass to Chad's lips and let the kid take a little sip from the drink. "Wow," Chad breathed after taking a drink. "That, um, is quite the, um drink."

"Yes, it is. Hopefully it will help to relax you. You seem very tense." Bart sat the drink down on the dresser they were standing beside. His hands slid over the silky fabric of the shirt Chad was wearing. His hands began to gently massage the tense shoulder muscles. "You need to relax, Chad. You are too tense."

"I, um, I, um am just an um…" Chad did not want to say he was nervous about doing a good job. Or about the fact that Bart was the first guest Chad had been assigned to. "I have just never been around a star like you before."

"Well, just relax, buddy," Bart said, rubbing Chad's back and shoulders. "I put my pants on one leg at a time just like you."

Bart moved in closer and pulled Chad back against him. Bart's strong arms pinning Chad to him as his fingers slid over Chad's chest and flat belly. The thin fabric of Chad's silk shirt was all that was separating Bart's fingers from Chad's smooth skin.

CHAD THOUGHT he could feel Bart's semi-erect manhood pressing against his butt. He was sure he could feel that male organ pressing against him. He knew he was feeling the heat of Bart's body soaking through his clothes. Bart's embrace was both warm and tender while also being distinctly sexual.

"I, um, Mr....um, I mean Bart."

"Shhh," Bart breathed into Chad's ear. "Just relax." Bart's fingers had already undone several buttons of Chad's shirt and he was now sliding his fingers inside the material. His fingertips were touching the soft, smooth skin of Chad's chest.

"Ooooh," Chad breathed at the warm touch. His body was tingling everywhere. The spots being touched by Bart's fingers were feeling like an electrical current was being sent into him.

"Mmmm, your skin is so soft and smooth," Bart breathed. His lips were next to Chad's ear. Then he moved his head slightly and soon he had Chad's earlobe in between his lips and began to softly nibble on it. His teeth and tongue were teasing the small piece of flesh.

"Oh gawd," Chad moaned. He could not believe how good this was all feeling. He had never felt anything like Bart's lips and mouth on his ear before. He had no idea that his earlobe was so sensitive.

Bart's fingers had finished unbuttoning Chad's shirt and had the silky material pulled open. His fingers were playing over Chad's body like Chad was the guitar that Bart often played on stage. His hand slid up from Chad's navel up to the smooth pectoral muscles. His fingers finding one of

"I, um, I, you, I am so um…"

"Fucking horny," Bart supplied.

Chad's cheeks grew warm but he nodded an ascent. He was horned up by the touch of this hot man. He had never been turned on so much in his life. The guy was gorgeous and his body was awesome. Then there was the fact that the man seemed to know exactly which buttons to push.

Bart's fingers had begun to unbutton and unzip Chad's black pants. His fingers were lowering the zipper and then slipping into the open folds of fabric.

"Oh gawd," Chad crooned as he felt the warmth of Bart's palm through the nylon fabric of his thong.

"Hmmm, what do we have here?" Bart asked, feeling over the soft slick fabric. "I think I need to get a better look at this."

Chad felt the pants being pushed down his legs. He felt Bart's hands sliding over his skin as they lowered his pants down. He did not have to be told to kick off his shoes and step out of the pants. His body seemed to understand that was what was to happen, so it did it without conscious thought from his brain. Chad's brain was focused on keeping track of each sensation on his body. He was focusing on memorizing how Bart's hands felt as they slid down his legs. He focused his attention on the touches and the caresses of those musician fingers.

"Damn, but you are so damn sexy," Bart said looking up at the almost naked teen. His warm eyes were drinking in the sight of the boy. His nose inhaled deeply of the clean scent of the skin. His hands were feeling the smooth tan legs as they slid up to grasp the firm round but cheeks.

"I, um, you are, this is…"

Chad did not have the words to describe what his body was feeling. He had never felt sensations like this before. He had never known sex with a guy like Bart could be so intense.

Bart looked over the evenly sun-kissed skin. His eyes were memorizing every inch of the boy's body. He looked up into Chad's color shifting eyes and then down over Chad's firm chest, smooth belly and the material that covered the teenage erection. That stiff teen member tented out the nylon fabric. It was the tent pole that was straining to push the gold material off the boy's body.

"I can't believe I am doing this with you. I can't believe we are doing this. I would have never guessed that you were, um, well, um…" Chad did not know if he should use the term gay. Some of the celebs, he had been told, were annoyed by being labeled gay.

"You never guessed that I might be into gay sex or sex with a hot sexy teen like you?" Bart asked as he slid his hands up and down Chad's legs.

Chad looked down into Bart's handsome face. His eyes meeting Bart's, his skin tingling with Bart's caresses. He liked having this man kneeling before him looking him over. He was a bit self-conscious, but he liked the attention. "Both I guess."

"There is just something I find more fun about sex with another man. It is more fulfilling to me. I still love my wife, but I need to feel the touch of another man's body from time to time. I also have a need to sometimes share the experience with someone young and still new to the subject of man to man pleasure. Or in our case, man-to-boy pleasure. How old are you really?"

Chad was a bit surprised by Bart's question. He gave him the only answer he could, "Eighteen."

Bart wondered if that was a truthful answer. The kid could be eighteen, but Bart thought he might be fibbing a bit.

Bart's hands had reached the golden fabric. His fingers stroking the teen rod hidden behind the material. "I am going to take this off of you now," Bart informed his new friend.

"Okay," Chad said but Bart had already begun to lower the material.

Bart slowly pulled it down revealing Chad's perfectly shaped seven-inch cut cock. The head was shiny from pre cum.

"Beautiful," Bart breathed as the teen's rod came into sight. The head glistening in the soft light of the room.

Bart lowered the thong and Chad stepped out of it. The guy stood there completely naked with Bart kneeling before him. Bart's eyes sliding over every inch of Chad's young sexy body.

"These pubes are so damn sexy," Bart said, running his fingers through the soft blonde curls that surrounded Chad's turgid member.

Chad felt his face grow warm. He had never had anyone admire him quite like this before. He had never had another man lust for him.

Bart's fingers moved below Chad's cock and cupped the balls hanging in the smooth scrotum. Bart's fingers softly massaging and stroking the soft skin of Chad's ballsack.

"Oooooh," Chad sighed as he felt Bart's fingers go to work on him.

Bart watched Chad's boyhood jump with each stroke of his fingers against the kid's sensitive sack. He watched as a drop of pre cum formed on the perfectly shaped cut head. He watched the teen fluid grow in size as Chad's balls produced more of the boy's nectar.

"Mmmmm," Bart moaned looking at the drop of pre cum getting larger and larger. Bart leaned in and inhaled the scent of the teen. He drunk in the smell and then flicked his tongue across the head of Chad's cock. His tongue picking up that drop of pre cum and tasting it and drinking it down into his belly.

"Oh fuck," Chad cried.

When Bart's lips closed around the rigid teen dick, Chad lost control. His hips bucked, his balls tingled and drew up into his body and his cock exploded. His whole body went rigid. His mind filled with a blast of pleasure unlike anything Chad had ever experienced before.

Bart was surprised but pleased with the hot warm fluid flooding into his mouth. He swallowed down mouthful after mouthful of hot teen cum. Jet after jet firing into his mouth and filling it up. It was almost too much for the crooner to handle. Some of the white fluid leaked from the corner of his mouth.

"Ararararararar, ouohohohohohoh, aiaiaiaiaiaiaia," Chad cried gripping Bart's head tightly in his hands as his body unloaded his seed.

IT WAS the longest orgasm Chad had ever experienced. He had never felt anything quite like the wave of pleasure that went through him. If it had not been for Bart's strong arms, Chad probably would have collapsed right there. His body had used up his strength to spray the inside of Bart's mouth with hot cum.

Chad's hands slid from the silky locks of Bart's brown hair to the star's shoulders. His fingers lightly feeling the muscles beneath the shirt that Bart was wearing.

"Oh, gawd, oh gawd," Chad chanted several times while trying to regain some control.

Bart sucked at the head of Chad's cock pulling every last vestige of cum from the shaft. He wanted to drain those hot nuts of every drop of hot seed.

"I, I can't believe it. I, I am so, so sorry Mr. Parsons."

Bart pulled his lips off the teen dick and looked up at the naked guy. "Just what the hell are you apologizing for? That tasted damn good, kid."

"I, I didn't mean to…It was just I couldn't stop it. I, I, if you want a different attendant…"

Bart stood up his hands holding onto the naked teen. His eyes looking into Chad's. His voice soft and tender as he spoke. "Chad, you are the one I want. I want you and I want your cum in my mouth. You gave me exactly what I wanted. You gave me a great load of hot teen seed."

Chad was surprised. He didn't know that Bart would want to drink his load. He found it hard to understand that this big star wanted to eat cum. He had figured that he would be the one blowing Bart and not the other way around. "You sure it is okay? I will…"

Bart stopped Chad's words with a kiss to the boy's lips. His mouth covering Chad's. His tongue pushing into Chad's mouth.

Chad could taste the cum on Bart's lips. He could taste the cum on Bart's tongue.

For long moments the kiss lasted without either of them wanting it to end. Bart's hands slid over Chad's back and down to squeeze the kid's firm round bubble butt.

As the kiss broke, Chad let his tongue play around Bart's lips and he licked the corners of Bart's mouth clear of any trace of sperm. He cleaned his new lover of any drop of white boy juice.

"Was that your first blow job?" Bart asked looking into Chad's face.

"Um, well, um…" Chad's words trailed off as he felt his face blushing.

"That is fine if it was. It explains why you shot off so quickly. I mean I am good at sucking cock, but I don't usually get a guy to blow that fast."

"You sucked cock before?"

Bart chuckled as he answered. "Yes. This isn't my first time. I like sex with guys. I meant it when I told you that earlier. I like sucking cock and having my cock sucked."

"Then, then could I suck your cock?"

Bart smiled his eyes twinkling as he answered. "Well since you asked so nicely, I think that could be arranged."

Chad looked down at the bulge in Bart's pants. The man's pole was trying to force its way out of the zipper. His tented jeans stretched out in the front with his lust for release with this kid.

"Should I, um, how do you, I don't…"

"Relax, Chad. Don't worry about this being your first time sucking cock. I'll teach you everything you need to know. Just come and sit on the bed."

Bart led Chad over to the bed and watched the naked youth watching him.

"You know, um, Mr. Parsons…"

"Chad, I just sucked your dick. I have your cum coating my stomach, so please call me Bart. I think we know each other well enough for you to drop the Mr. Parsons."

"Um, yes, um, Bart. I was just saying that you are hotter than I ever imagined. I mean I have seen you perform and listened to you a bit but never knew you were this good looking."

Bart could see the kid's face blushing with his words. He wondered if Chad realized that he was the hottest kid Bart had seen in a long long time. "Chad, you are just as hot if not hotter. Your hair and eyes are stunning and your face is perfect. Your body is sexy and you taste great." Bart's smile helped relax Chad a little bit. "Now just relax and let me teach you even more about guy to guy fun."

Chad watched as Bart began to unbutton his shirt. His fingers making quick work of the buttons and he pulled the shirt open revealing his tan chest. The defined pectoral muscles and flat abdominal muscles showing that Bart worked out. Chad's eyes glided over Bart's torso and down to the man's belly button. His eyes noticing the dark hairs that begun just under that indentation and disappeared down into Bart's tight fitting pants. The front of those pants showing that Bart was generously endowed.

"Want to see more?" Bart asked enjoying the feeling of the kid looking him over.

"Yes," Chad said honestly.

Bart reached down and popped the button of his pants. He lowered the zipper and let the folds of fabric fall open. His white boxer briefs being revealed to the young man sitting naked on the bed before him. Bart turned showing Chad his back. The broad shoulders tapering down to his trim waist. Bart lowered the pants letting Chad look on at his underwear covered butt. His two muscled cheeks were stretching out the tight fitting CK boxer briefs.

Bart looked back over his shoulder watching the younger man looking at his body. He watched Chad watch him. Chad's hand had moved to his cock and was slowly stroking the wet organ as he watched Bart step out of the pants. His firm butt cheeks flexing beneath the underwear as he moved.

Bart slowly lowered the back waistband of his briefs. The tan skin of his ass coming into view for the horny teen. Lower and lower Bart moved the fabric watching Chad's eyes drink in the site of him.

Chad saw Bart's crack and then more and more of the two firm muscled cheeks. The skin of Bart's ass was not as dark as the other parts of his body, but Chad had a desire to touch those two cheeks. He had a need to push his face between them and drink in the smell and taste of Bart.

Bart stepped out of his boxer briefs and stood there for a moment completely naked with his back to Chad. Bart ran a hand over his chest and played with his nipples feeling his cock jump and twitch as he teased his tits. He could not wait for Chad to suck on his chest or for Chad to suck his cock. He knew the kid was going to enjoy it. He was going to love the taste of his dick.

Bart slowly turned around. Chad couldn't believe this man was standing here in front of him completely naked. He looked up at Bart's handsome face as Bart turned around. He looked into Bart's eyes and smiled. Then his gaze slid down over Bart's chest and down over the flat abs again. He could not wait to feel his body against Bart's. He could not wait to feel that warm body rubbing against his with nothing between them but skin.

Chad's eyes moved down into Bart's dark pubic thatch. The dark curls surrounding Bart's tool. Chad's eyes got large and his mouth dropped open as he looked at the large tool.

"Do you like what you see?" Bart asked running a hand down over his chest and belly. His fingers moved into his brown pubic hair and went around the base of his thick tool. "Do you want to play with this kid?"

Chad looked at the hard dick. He watched it move left and right as Bart slowly shook it at Chad. Chad looked up and down the long length of the tool. The thick shaft with the vein running up the side from the base to the large cut mushroom head. The long shaft curved up and to the right. "I, I, um, well, it is kind of big."

"Yeah, a bit," Bart said looking down at his own dick. "But I think you will enjoy playing with it. I think you will like what it can do."

Bart took a few steps closer to Chad. His thick dick moving as he stepped closer to the kid who was still staring at his cock. He smiled at the blonde teen as he said, "Go on, Chad, touch it. Wrap your fingers around it and give it a squeeze. Come on play with my dick. I know you want too."

Chad had touched a few other dicks before but never on a celebrity or one that was so big. He and his friend Brent use to play with each other's cocks, but Brent did not have anything like this.

Chad's fingers touched the warm flesh. His hand and fingers feeling the heat radiating from Bart's tool.

"Yeah, that is it," Bart said softly. "Go on and wrap your hand around me. Mmmmm, your touch feels so good, Chad. Your fingers are so soft as they touch my skin."

Chad's fingers slid over the head and around the crown. Then with one finger tip, Chad traced the vein that pulsed to Bart's regular heartbeat. When Chad's fingers reached the base of Bart's perfect piece of male flesh, they encircled the thick shaft and began to slowly slide up and down the hardness. "It's so big. I knew that some guys had big equipment. I mean, I think I am a bit above average, but this…"

"I am glad you like it. You can play with it as much as you want. Go ahead and explore it, Chad. Let your fingers memorize every inch of me. Let them know how my cock curves and throbs."

Chad did as the studly man instructed. He slid his fingers up and down the shaft. He memorized the hot and hard organ. He ran a finger over the head and through the piss slit. The eye of Bart's cock leaking the smallest drop of pre cum as Chad slid his finger through the piss slit.

"Would you like to try sucking it?" Bart asked the teen.

"I, I think you are too big," Chad said studying the dick that was suspended above two very large eggs.

"I think you can handle it. Go on and just start out by licking with your tongue. Pretend it is a big ice pop and lick it. Go on, Chad, lick it."

Chad leaned in and kissed the head of Bart's cock. His tongue and lips making contact with the sensitive skin of Bart's head. His tongue seeming to know what to do as it began to guide Chad over the head and down the side of the cock. Then it slid up the other side of the cock back to the head. All around the crown Chad licked. Then under the crown, he slid his tongue from the underside of the head all the way down to where Bart's ballsack connects with his dick.

"Ooooooh, damn Chad, you feel good. Now go on and put it into your mouth. Just be careful with your teeth."

Chad sat back for a moment and looked at the now wet and shiny dick. His hand still barely able to fully encircle the male organ.

"I'll do my best," Chad told Bart before leaning forward and putting his lips around the head of the dick.

"Aaaaaah," Bart sighed as Chad popped his head into the warm wetness of the kid's mouth.

"Easy does it," Bart said as Chad began to slowly move over the head and down the shaft of the big dick. "Take your time. I am not going to go anywhere. We have all the time in the world." Bart slid his fingers through the soft golden curls that covered Chad's head. The soft silkiness of the kid's hair causing Bart's cock to jump and twitch.

"Mmmmmm," Chad moaned as he held onto Bart's muscular legs and sucked more of the thick dick into his mouth.

"Ahahahah," Bart sighed as Chad took more of the length into his mouth. "Watch the teeth," Bart breathed as his cock was scraped by Chad's inexperienced mouth.

"Sorry," Chad said pulling off the wet dick and looking up at Bart. "Should I stop?"

"No way, kid. Just take your time and be a little more careful."

Chad moved back down to Bart's cock. His lips moving around the head and slowly moving down over the shaft. He took his time and kept his teeth from scraping the sensitive male organ.

"You are doing great," Bart breathed between closed eyes. His body was tingling with the pleasure of the hot kid's mouth.

Chad's lips moved closer to the base of Bart's cock. His mouth filled with the large meat. His own dick was harder than Chad could ever remember it being and it was dripping new pre cum onto the bed.

"That feels so good," Bart said rubbing Chad's bare shoulders and silky golden locks. "Try to go all the way down. Just take your time and when you feel my head at your throat swallow as you move forward on the shaft."

Chad pushed his mouth further down Bart's blood filled cock. His throat contracted and caused him to choke. He gagged and coughed and pulled back with his eyes watering.

"Take it easy, champ," Bart said rubbing Chad's shoulders again. "It takes some practice to get it just right."

"I'm sorry I am not better at this," Chad said blushing and feeling annoyed with himself.

"Hey, man," that is just fine buddy," Bart said looking down into Chad's cute face. "You will get the hang of it. Just give it another try. Take your time and suck me down."

Chad did as Bart instructed and swallowed down on Bart's cock again. He gagged and forced the reflex down. It took all of his effort but after several more attempts, he had the head of Bart's cock in his throat.

"Oh gawd," Bart groaned as Chad's throat muscles stroked his cock head. "It feels wonderful, buddy."

Chad was using all of his self-control not to choke on the oversized organ. He pushed forward and more of Bart's thickness filled his throat. More and more Chad swallowed down Bart's tool.

"Oh, oh shit," Bart groaned. "You have just about done it. I am just about ready to blow."

Chad slid his mouth forward taking in another inch of the man's penis. He swallowed as the dick slid down into his throat. He gripped Bart's legs with his hands as he sucked up and down on Bart. His lips stroking the shaft and his tongue teasing the head.

"Oh yeah, you learn fast kid. You are sucking cock like a pro."

Bart's words gave Chad a little more confidence and he sucked a little faster and began to bob up and down on Bart's tool. His tongue was swirling around the cock and his lips were getting tickled by the brown pubic hair when Chad moved forward.

Bart could feel his balls pulling up. He could feel the cum beginning to move from inside him. He could feel the heat of his cock increase. He knew it would only take a moment more. It would only take one more second.

Chad felt Bart's cock get thicker. He actually believed it got longer as well. He could not believe how much of the stud he had in his mouth. There was not much of Bart's cock left outside Chad's mouth.

"Oh gawd yes, I am gonna…"

Bart's fingers were teasing his erect nipples, his balls were pulled up tight and he was sliding over the edge into orgasmic pleasure.

"Chad, if you don't want a mouth full of cum, you had better pull off now," Bart said panting as he tried to hold back his climax.

Chad kept right on sucking his new friend. He wanted to taste Bart's load. He wanted Bart to give him that hot seed.

"Ahahahahahaah, ieieieieieieeie, ohohohohohoh!!!"

Bart's cock erupted in Chad's mouth. His cock jumping as it fired salvo after salvo into Chad's hungry mouth. The huge load soon filling Chad's mouth beyond what the kid could handle.

Bart gripped the teen firmly as he rode the intense wave of pleasure. His cock jumping as it shot the jets of hot white seed into Chad's mouth. His balls emptying themselves of the stored up cum. He had been waiting for this for a long time and the release was better than he had been imagining.

Chad swallowed down the cum Bart shot but there was just too much of it for him to handle. He soon had cum leaking from the corners of his mouth and dripping off his chin. He swallowed and sucked but it seemed like Bart's balls would never finish emptying themselves.

Finally, Bart's cock stopped his torrential deluge of Chad's mouth and the star stepped back. His cock plopping from Chad's lips with a wet slurping sound. "That was one of the best blow jobs I have ever had."

Bart flopped down on the bed. His body weak after the powerful orgasm. "You have no idea how good that felt, Chad."

Chad had not moved when Bart had flopped on the bed. His naked tan body was looking very sexy with the semi-erect cock glistening in the soft light of the bedroom.

"I, um, am glad it was okay," Chad said looking back toward the floor with Bart on the bed behind him.

Bart reached out and with a strong arm around Chad, he pulled the teen back onto the bed. His fingers tenderly stroking the soft skin of the younger man.

Chad allowed himself to be pulled and maneuvered on the bed. He soon found he was lying beside Bart with his head on Bart's shoulder. His body stretched out beside the sexy guy.

"You were better than just okay," Bart said stroking Chad's back as he spoke. "It was your first time, but you did great for a first time and I can only imagine what you will be like when you perfect your cock sucking ability."

"I just can't believe you enjoyed it after me being stupid and scraping you with my teeth."

"Hey, you are not stupid buddy. You are cute, sexy and you seem smart. You just need to practice sucking dick. Plus you started out on a cock that is a bit above average."

"You are a bit larger than I expected," Chad said. "I can't believe a stud like you has not been sucked off by the world's best cock sucker."

"I have had a lot of blow jobs, by both women and guys and yours was by far one of the best. It wasn't the best one ever but it was up in the top five. You will only get better."

"Thanks, um, Bart."

"Chad, I would like to ask you something, and I hope you don't mind me being so, um, interested. You don't have to answer if you don't want to though. It is entirely up to you."

"Okay. I'll try and be as truthful as I can."

"Have you ever had any kind of sex with anybody before me?"

"Well, um, I, um..." Chad's face turned bright red. He did not want to admit the truth, but decided that there was really no harm. "A friend and I use to jerk each other off, but nothing other than that.

"So this was the first time you had given a blow job or received one."

"Yes," Chad answered.

"Have you ever had sex with a girl?"

"Um, well," Again, Chad decided to be honest with his new lover. "No I haven't. I, um, just don't find them much of a turn on."

"But you find me a turn on, don't you?" Bart asked rolling over on top of Chad. Bart's naked body pressed against the young guys. Their two dicks sticking to each other from the spit and pre cum that covered them.

"I, um, well, hell yes, Bart. You're fucking hot. You're damn sexy. You're great and so much more."

"Good," Bart said leaning down and kissing Chad's soft lips. His tongue licking the cum from them. Then Bart went to lick Chad's cheeks and chin clean of the cum that had leaked out of Chad's mouth. Bart was basically licking his cum off of Chad's face.

Chad's cock was rock hard again and pressing against Bart's firm body. It wanted to experience more, it wanted to find out all of the pleasure that two men could bring to each other.

Bart supported most of his weight on his elbows. He did not want to crush the youth that lay beneath him. He wanted to give Chad pleasure and to receive pleasure from the youth.

Chad's arm went around Bart. His hands feeling the soft skin and tracing the firm muscles of Bart's back. He wanted to stay like this for days. His teen rod was rock hard now and pushing into Bart.

After long minutes of kissing and caressing, Bart rolled to lay beside Chad with his arm holding the youth tight. There two bodies curling up to rest and recover.

They both drifted off snoozing and resting. Both of them getting ready for a second round of guy to guy action.

BART AWOKE first to find the naked youth snoring softly in his arms. They were spooned up against each other with Chad's bubble butt pressing against Bart's soft member. His dick had deflated during the night, but he knew it would not take much to bring it back to being fully erect.

He quietly slid out of the bed and strode naked to the bathroom. He stood relieving his bladder. His body feeling better than it had in quite a while. He slept better with Chad in his arms that he had in weeks. He knew that this trip would give him the rest and relaxation he needed.

Bart shook the last few drops off of his cock and then washed his hands. He then went into the sitting room and made a call to the front desk. He knew that the two of them would need large amounts of food in a few hours. They were going to work up quite a hunger.

Then Bart slid back into bed but not before grabbing a bottle out of the night stand.

Bart kissed the back of Chad's head and ran his hand softly down along the sleeping form. His fingers were lightly caressing the soft teenage skin. He found the crack of Chad's cheeks and slipped his fingers between those two solid orbs of muscle. Bart pushed the flip top lid on the bottle of lube up with his thumb. He then pulled his hand back from touching Chad so he could put a generous amount of the slick substance onto his finger.

Bart pushed Chad's legs apart a bit and began to do a slow hunt for Chad's virgin boy hole. He found the tight anal ring and began to slowly rub his slick finger around the opening.

"Wha, what are you doing?" Chad asked slowly waking up from the best night's sleep he had for quite a while.

"Just lubing up your tight little back door."

"I, um, I um…"

Relax, man," Bart said leaning in close and kissing the teen's shoulder. His lips traveling up to nip at Chad's ear as his finger pushed inside Chad's body.

"Ohohohohoh," Chad groaned as his anal opening was stretched for the first time. "It hurts a bit."

"I know it does, babe," Bart said as he kissed more of Chad's soft skin. "But it will get better. Trust me."

Chad felt Bart's finger sliding in and out of his ass. He could feel the sexy guy pushing it in deeper and deeper. He could feel the sensation slowly changing from one of pain to a mixed of pain and intense pleasure. The pleasure seeming even sweeter after the pain.

"Oh, oh, Bart," Chad breathed as his dick began throbbing and dripping pre cum onto the sheet.

"Feeling better isn't it?"

"Oh, yeah, the pain is going away and it feels good."

"Just wait," Bart said and turned his finger a bit. He then pushed in a little more and found that hard gland that was Chad's prostate. He rubbed his finger against that button and heard the sharp intake of breath and the whimper of pleasure from his new lover. "You like that huh?"

"Oh, oh, oh, oh, ahahahahahaha," Chad moaned louder.

Bart's cock was rock hard and dripping his own pre cum juices onto the bedding. He could not wait to introduce this hot kid to the pleasure of anal penetration. His cock jumped with the thought of being inside of this virgin butt.

"Chad, I am going to add a second finger. I want to loosen you up and get you ready for the best thing you have felt yet." Bart pulled his finger from Chad's hole and squeezed lube onto two of them. He then pushed the first finger and a second one into the tight sphincter. His fingers stretching Chad more than before.

"Ohohoh, ohohoh it hurts again," Chad groaned in pain.

"Just relax. You know it is going to get better." Bart massaged the anal ring working his fingers left and right loosing up his younger friend. His finger occasionally fining Chad's prostate and pushing against it. He would hear a whimper when he did that and knew that Chad was enjoying the butt play that Bart was performing.

Bart added a third finger and this time there was just the smallest of added groans from his friend. The kid was definitely learning to enjoy the pleasure that only one man knows how to give to another man. Bart's three fingers stretched and massaged the tight anal opening. His fingers sliding in easily after a few minutes of work. He wondered just how receptive this kid's ass was going to be to his big cock. He knew many guys were very intimidated by his nine-inch member and that some just did not want to try to take something that was as thick as his tool up inside them. Chad however seemed willing to experience anything Bart wanted him to experience.

Bart added a forth finger to Chad's butt and nibbled on his shoulder as Chad began to push back against Bart's fingers. "Ah, I do think you are enjoying getting finger fucked."

"Oh, gawd, Bart. Oh gawd."

Bart moved his mouth to Chad's shoulder, kissing him. Then to Chad's neck. His teeth and mouth were working on Chad's neck marking him with a hicky.

After only a couple more minutes, Bart decided he could wait no longer and that Chad was ready for more than just a few fingers in his butt.

He removed his fingers from the now receptive opening. He then moved Chad onto his back and into the center of the bed. Bart moved over Chad stretching out on top of the young man and kissing his lips and chin and neck. "You are just so damn sexy," Bart breathed next to Chad's ear.

Chad's arms automatically wrapped around Bart. His hands feeling the solidness of the man's back and the firmness of the guy's ass cheeks. Chad never wanted Bart to move. It felt so good having the warm weight of this superstar on top of him. He wondered just how much more pleasure there was to come from this man.

Using his knees, Bart pushed Chad's legs apart. He spread the guy open and moved between the stretched out legs. Sitting back up between Chad's legs, Bart looked down at the naked young man. He looked at the solid pole of teen flesh that pointed skyward. He looked at the hunger in the blue green eyes of the teen.

"I want to fuck you," Bart said looking at the guy that was going to give Bart his virginity.

"And I want you to do it to me."

Bart grabbed the lubricant and squeezed some into the palm of his hand. He then applied the generous amount of lubricant to his dick. He slicked himself up stroking his hard dick with a hand and then lifting Chad's legs up and back over the young man's body.

Bart looked down at the puckered rose bud just waiting to be penetrated for the first time. He moved in closer and touched that puckered hole with the head of his slicked up dick. He then looked into Chad's eyes. "You ready for this?"

"Yes, I am. Put it inside me."

Bart pushed his dick against the tight opening. Even after the time and care Bart had put into getting Chad's ass ready for this, the boy was still tight. Bart's thick cut cock head stretched the opening wider and wider. Bart pushed hard and harder so he felt the head of his large organ pushed into the opening. He felt those anal lips making a tight seal around his invading cock. He felt Chad's pain and could read it on Chad's face.

"It hurts," Chad said.

Bart left his dick rest just inside the opening. He wanted to give this hot guy a chance to get used to having a dick in his ass. He knew the kid would soon want more than just the tip of the dick. He would want all of those nine inches.

"I know it hurts," Bart said leaning down, "But it will get better." Bart placed a soft kiss on Chad's lips and also pushed a little bit more of his length into Chad. His dick pushing forward and stretching Chad's anal muscles.

"Ohohohohoh," Chad sighed with the pain. His fists gripping the bed clothes.

Bart rested there for a few moments to give the muscles time to adjust to the thickness. He then slowly pushed more of the tool into Chad. The nine inches now only showing six inches outside of Chad's body. The other three inch securely inserted into Chad's ass.

"We are almost half way there, buddy," Bart said letting the boy rest again.

"Damn you're fucking big," Chad said breathing hard. "You are fucking big."

"You will soon be happy that my dick is big. You will soon enjoy those inches of dick sliding in and out."

Bart was already pushing his dick back and forth and left and right. He was working it slowly so that Chad would get use to the length and thickness. In and out Bart worked his cock. Each time he went a little bit deeper on the in-thrust. Each time making Chad's ass accept more man meat.

Bart could feel Chad's anal muscles relaxing so he pushed hard and drove another inch into Chad. He had well over half his dick inside the tight hole. In just a few more thrust Bart would be fully imbedded in the boy's tight ass.

Chad felt the tickle of Bart's thick pubes against his skin. He knew that Bart must just about be all the way inside him. It hurt to have this big dick inside of him, but it also felt good. Chad could not believe he had gotten this hot stud to fuck him. He could not believe how lucky he was to have found this job and to be with this amazing guy. Sometimes celebrities had the reputation of being a nice guy but more often than not, they were all stuck on themselves and were jerks. Chad was learning that it did not appear to be that way with Bart. Bart actually seemed to care about Chad enjoying every part of this experience. Chad could not have asked for a better way to give up his virginity.

The pain that Bart's dick was causing him was almost completely gone now. In fact, there were intense waves of pleasure coming from the organ. Chad could feel each thick inch of Bart's dick and every time the stud moved it in and out he could feel a sharp wave of pleasure pass through him. It almost made him blast his teen cum all over the two of them.

"I'm all the way inside of you," Bart said. "You have all of my length buried inside that tight ass. How does it feel now?"

"It's, it's different. It's good. It's great. You are great."

"Good," Bart said leaning forward to place a hard kiss on Chad's lips. Bart drove his tongue into Chad's mouth and began to slowly pull out and push in Chad's ass. In and out Bart moved his cock. His dick rubbing the inside walls of Chad's anal chute as Bart began a slow and steady fuck.

"I'm not too deep am I?" Bart asked.

"Oh gawd no. You're fucking great. I love it man. I love it."

Bart rested Chad's legs on his shoulders and then leaned forward again. His lips kissing and his tongue licking the hot young man. His arms on either side of the hot and horny teen as he began to fuck the kid harder. Bart's tool thrusting deep in and out. Almost all of his length sliding in and out of Chad. Every inch of Bart's pleasure rod driving up to the hilt into Chad's ass.

Instinctively, Chad began flexing his anal muscles as Bart fucked him. He squeezed hard as that cock tried to pull out and relaxed as it pushed back inside. The two seemed to be in perfect unison as they fucked. In and out. Chad's hands gripped Bart's arms firmly as he let the superstar fuck him. Chad's fingers sliding up over the hard cords of muscle that made up Bart's arms.

"Oh Bart, oh gawd, I think I am going to cum," Chad said.

"Ahahahahahaha, ohohohohohohohoh," Chad cried as his cock began firing cum all over the two men. Ropes of hot white teen seed splattered across Bart's tan skin. Rope after rope sticking to Bart's skin.

"Yeah, shoot it man. Shoot your hot load of cream, Chad. Shoot that shit all over me. Fucking cum, kid, cum!"

Bart's voice was loud and demanding and it was obvious the mature guy was enjoying the session as much as anyone.

Bart could feel his balls tightening up. He knew he was close to blowing a massive load of real seed into Chad's ass. He knew it would not take long and he would be coming.

"Aiaiaiaiaiaiaiaiaiaiaiaiaaia, oaoaoaoaoaoaoaoaoaoaoaao," Bart yelled as he began shooting his cream into Chad. "Take that fucking load, kid, take all my seed into your ass!"

Bart's big nine-inch tool fired the ropes of cum from Bart's huge nuts into Chad's guts. Jet after jet of hot seed was being driven deep up into Chad by the powerful spasms of Bart's cock. "Ohohohohohoh fuck yesesesesesesess!"

Bart's body was tensed up. His skin was covered with a glistening sheen of sweat. His muscles were popping out as he rode the waves of pleasure.

Chad's hands slid over Bart's slick sweat-covered body. His fingers feeling the solid steel cords of muscle that covered Bart's arms, shoulders, back and chest. He licked and sucked on Bart's right nipple as the stud dumped gallons of seed into his ass.

The wave of pleasure seemed to last forever but was over far too soon. Bart fell forward on top of Chad and let the younger man hold him tight. Their two sweaty bodies glued together with the fluids they had each produced. Bart's cock slowly growing soft but still firmly planted inside Chad.

They lay there breathing hard and holding each other, their bodies stuck together by cum, sweat and Bart's cock still firmly gripped by the teen's tight no-longer-virgin butt.

THE END

Here is a sample from another story you may enjoy:

KEITH YATES

Blind
ATTRACTIONS

GAY ROMANCE EROTICA

LET'S FIRST give you a little background. I am a widower at the ripe old age of 45. My wife died of Cancer about seven years ago. It came on her quite suddenly. We went through the battle with radiation and the whole bit but within six months she was gone. It was a rough year for me. I loved her a great deal and still do. We got married young and it was not until after our wedding that I really understood that I had feelings, sexual feelings, toward other men.

I have brown hair and eyes. I am clean shaven, around 5 feet 10 inches tall and have a slender runners built. I live in a quiet neighborhood of our city. It is near the park where I often go for long walks with my dog. The neighborhood is old and very nice to live and raise a family. All of the people are great to live nearby. Everyone is friendly and considerate.

The house across the street from mine had been for sale for about a year. The family that lived there had moved out and the place was in the hands of a real estate agency. I noticed one day that the "for sale" sign was finally gone. It looked like I was going to get new neighbors. I just hoped that they would be good neighbors.

I was taking Lenny, my dog, for a walk the first time I saw him. He was carrying boxes from a van into the house. He looked like an average guy. He was attractive with wavy brown hair. He was wearing dark sunglasses so I couldn't see his eyes. He was a couple inches taller than me and looked fit. He had a friend helping him move and they seemed to be pretty busy. I thought if I caught them taking a break on the way back I would go over and introduce myself and Lenny.

Lenny and I walked through the park and he did his normal business. He sniffed, he peed and then he pooped. Over the past year or so, I had caught myself looking more and more at the men in the park. Many people came to the park to exercise. There were always runners, joggers, walkers, bicyclists and skate boarders in the park. I had noticed that many of the guys were very attractive. I found myself looking over the exposed skin of these athletic men. I was beginning to check out their arms, muscular chests, lean legs, firm butts and the packages they had in their shorts. I had not acted on my sexual feelings for other men. I was not exactly sure how to go about it. I mean could you just go up to a guy in the park and flirt or did you need to be more blunt. I watched a guy I had seen before in the park. He was running in a pair of tight fitting shorts and no shirt. His chest was broad and mostly smooth except for a patch of hair between the two pectorals. His skin was tan and his muscles were well defined and bulged as he ran. I had noticed him before wearing dog tags so guessed him to be either active or former military. I just knew he was attractive and had an awesome body. I could feel my penis beginning to respond to the sight of him and decided I had better head back before I got too erect.

I turned the corner out of the park and began the walk home. I had to pass by the house on the corner and as I walked past the front I noticed the man that had been carrying boxes earlier on the front porch. His back was to me and I decided to go welcome him to the neighborhood. "Hi there," I said as I got to the bottom of the steps. He had already begun to turn in my direction as he had heard me approach. It was when he turned that I noticed the white cane in his right hand. I was surprised to say the least.

"Hello," he greeted.

"My name is Ben," I said. "I live next door." I had raised my hand and pointed and then realized how stupid that was as he couldn't see where I was pointing. "I mean right over there."

He smiled at me and pointed in the direction of my house. "Is that over there?" he asked and was grinning.

"Um, yes. Sorry," I said. I could feel my embarrassment on my neck and was glad he couldn't see it.

"No big deal," he said. "I get that all the time. Left or right work better. North, South, East and West work even better. My name is Kent," he said and held out his hand.

I took it and shook it firmly. He seemed like a nice guy to me. He was better looking than I had originally thought. He was also in good shape. His tee shirt was clinging to his chest and his arms were well muscled and the forearms were covered with a fine layer of dark hair. He was a handsome man in his late twenties or early thirties. "So are you moving in?" I asked.

"Yes, I closed on the house a week or so ago and my friend is helping me move some of my stuff. The movers are coming tomorrow with the big items. He is in there on the phone talking to his girlfriend. I am hoping he keeps it short."

"Yes, I understand. I am sure you have a great deal of work to get done today," I said. I glanced down over his legs and lower body and could not help but notice how the blue jeans were clinging to his well - muscled legs and that he filled them out very nicely. I then saw Lenny at his feet sniffing his shoes. He looked down as if he could see the dog and I explained. "That is Lenny, my pup. We were just coming back from a walk."

"Oh," he said and leaned down to scratch Lenny's ears. The dog was in heaven as Kent found one of Lenny's favorite spots to be scratched. Lenny moved around behind Kent and he turned to scratch the pup again. Now I was getting an excellent view of his tight butt in those tight fitting jeans. They hugged each cheek and I had the urge to reach out and touch them.

"He's a great dog," Kent said turning back around to me.

"Oh, yes, he is," I said trying to hide my erection. Then I realized it did not matter. At least it did not matter until his friend came out the door.

"You finally off the phone?" Kent asked.

"Yes," he answered. "She is going to drive me crazy."

"John, this is Ben, Ben this is my buddy John," Kent said. We shook hands.

"I think I should go and let you too get back to work," I said. "Welcome to the neighborhood."

They both said they would see me later and they went back to work and I went back to my house across the street. I would see them from time to time during the afternoon. I was impressed at how Kent carried just as many boxes and furniture as his buddy. Kent was the better looking of the two in my opinion. John was handsome. He had blue eyes and sandy blonde hair. His body had a wiry build and he was not as tan as Kent. They worked long into the day making different trips from where Kent had been living to his new home. It was interesting to watch Kent carry boxes without his cane. He took his time at first but I guess as he learned the paths from the van better he moved faster. If they carried something that was too big for just one of them, John would lead and Kent would follow without any problem. I considered taking them over both a beer or two but wasn't sure if they drank or not. I did not want to make a bad impression on my new neighbor.

I could easily see Kent's house from mine. I would often see him leaving for work in the morning and then again in the evening when he got home. He would walk past my house to get to the bus stop. I often watched just because he was pleasant to watch. I found myself growing more and more fascinated with him. Whenever I saw him outside and I was outside I would make a point of going across the street and saying hello. He was always friendly and we would talk for several minutes sometimes up to an hour just there in his yard. Lenny loved it when I would stop at Kent's after or before one of our walks. Kent would sometimes have a dog treat for the little beggar.

Several weeks went by with me chatting with Kent and Lenny sniffing him all over. Too bad I could not stick my nose in some of the places Lenny had. I was getting ready for work one morning and looked out my bedroom window to see what the weather was doing. It was cloudy, but didn't look like it was going to rain yet. I glanced at Kent's house and saw that the curtains to one of his bedroom windows were slightly parted. I watched for a minute and that was when he walked in front of the window. He was wearing only his briefs. I caught just a glimpse of his body and it was not enough for me. I wanted to see more. I wanted him to stand there in front of his bedroom window and undress for me. Unfortunately that did not happen. I went on to work, but while I was out at lunch, I picked up a set of binoculars. The kind I purchased was for bird watching, so it should be a feasible cover if someone should find me with them. I then hurried back home and looked through my window. Sure enough Kent's curtain was still parted. I was sure he had forgotten about it. I was certain he had opened the window to let in fresh air and had forgotten to pull the curtain.

I looked through the binoculars and could see better into his bedroom. The room was dark and I still did not have much of a view. I just hoped that it would be enough to let me see more of him.

I think at this point it is obvious that I had become a bit obsessed with the man. He seemed to project some sort of sexuality that I was drawn to. I was like a moth being pulled into the flame. I wondered how badly I would get burned.

If you enjoyed this sample then look for **Blind Attractions**.

Also by this Author

Blind Attractions

About the Author

Keith Yates currently lives in Memphis, TN. He is a fan of many genres of writing including drama, camp, sci-fi, supernatural, etc.

From the Author

Check my page on Amazon for Updates and interesting info.

Author Central - http://www.amazon.com/Keith-Yates/e/B005X917G4

If you enjoyed any of my books then please share the love and click like on my books in Amazon.

If you write me a review and send me an email I will send you a free book, or many.
(Just know that these emails are filtered by my publisher.)

Good news is always welcome.

One Last Thing, For Kindle Readers...

When you turn the page, Kindle will give you the opportunity to rate this book and share your thoughts on Facebook and Twitter. If you enjoyed my writings, would you please take a few seconds to let your friends know about it? Because... when they enjoy they will be grateful to you and so will I.

Thank You!

Keith Yates
keith_yates@awesomeauthors.org